H.E. BE

For Jillian Hulme Gilliland
Mary Alice Downie

In memory of Bess and Jiggs.
Muriel Wood

Scared Sarah

By Mary Alice Downie

with illustrations by Muriel Wood

Published in Canada by Fitzhenry & Whiteside,
195 Allstate Parkway, Markham, Ontario L3R 4T8

Published in the United States by Fitzhenry & Whiteside,
121 Harvard Avenue, Suite 2, Allston, Massachusetts 02134

www.fitzhenry.ca   godwit@fitzhenry.ca.
10 9 8 7 6 5 4 3 2 1

National Library of Canada Cataloguing in Publication Data

Downie, Mary Alice, 1934 - Scared Sarah

(New beginnings)
ISBN 1-55041-712-6 (bound).--ISBN 1-55041-714-2 (pbk.)

1. Ontario--History--1791-1841--Juvenile fiction. 2. Ojibwa Indians--Juvenile fiction.
3. Frontier and pioneer life--Ontario--Juvenile fiction. 4. Fear--Juvenile fiction.
I. Wood, Muriel II. Title. III. Series: New beginnings (Markham, Ont.)

PS8557.O85S3 2002   jC813'.54   C2002-900021-1
PZ7.D75924Sa 2002

U.S. Publisher Cataloging-in-Publication Data
(Library of Congress Standards)

Downie, Mary Alice.
Scared Sarah / by Mary Alice Downie : illustrated by Muriel Wood. -- 1st ed.
[64] p. : col. ill. ; cm. (New Beginnings)
Summary: Living in the wilds of Upper Canada in 1836, Sarah is afraid of everything. She visits the
Ojibwa encampment, where she becomes friends with the chief's son and learns of his medicine
bag, full of magic for bravery and protection that she wants for herself.
ISBN 1-55041-712-6   ISBN 1-55041-714-2 (pbk.)
1. Friends -- Fiction. 2. Fear -- Fiction. I. Wood, Muriel . II. Title. III. Series.
[E] 21 2002   AC CIP

Fitzhenry & Whiteside acknowledges with thanks the Canada Council for the Arts, the Government
of Canada through the Book Publishing Industry Development Program (BPIDP), and the Ontario
Arts Council for their support for our publishing program.

Design by Wycliffe Smith Design

Table of Contents

CHAPTER 1

The Meanest Brothers

"Stop sniveling or your nose will wash away."
Sarah mopped her tears and touched her nose gently to make sure it was still there.

"You're afraid of your own shadow," said Tom.

"Girls are always afraid," said Jack. "All I did was put a little snake in her pocket."

"Tom, Jack, come with me. We have logs to chop," called their father. "Stop teasing your sister."

"Coming, Papa." Jack picked up his axe and strode out the door. The snake slithered into the corner, gently hissing.

"I'm sorry he frightened you, Sarah," Tom said with a kindly smile. "Here's a present to make you feel better."

"Thank you, Tom." Sarah took the small box from her brother's hand. It was made from birch bark and was tied with green reeds. She undid the reeds and raised the lid. A fat, warty toad jumped out. Sarah screamed. Laughing, the boys ran off to catch up with their father.

Sarah's mother was stirring wild cranberries in a big pot over the open fire. "What have they done to you now, Sarah?" she asked.

Sarah just sobbed.

"They'll keep teasing you until you become brave. Once they see you're no longer afraid, they'll stop their silly games."

"I have the meanest brothers in the whole world!" Sarah cried. "Sisters too," she added, remembering the day before. Her big sister Susanna and her little sister Caroline had hidden behind the woodpile and jumped out at her when she had gone for more kindling for the fire.

"You should have seen mine!" laughed her mother. "Now dry your eyes and fetch your shawl. As soon as I've finished with these preserves, you can come with me to the Ojibwa encampment. I need more baskets to store vegetables in the root cellar for the winter. Maybe, just maybe, there might be new moccasins for you. Your toes are poking out of the pair you have now."

Feeling more cheerful, Sarah ran for her shawl. She was happy most of the time. She liked living in the snug log house with her mother, father, two brothers and two sisters. The walls were covered with her mother's paintings of wild roses and violets, snowbirds and dear little screech owls with surprised expressions on their faces. There was a vegetable garden, a herb garden and pots of red geraniums on the window ledge.

All the trees had been chopped down beside the house, but there were still stumps everywhere. And there was a fence made out of fallen logs with branches and brush on top.

Sarah's kitten, Ruff, had a circle of white fur around his neck. Her little sister Caroline had a tame pigeon called Coo-coo. Her brother Jack's pet snake, Sippet, had beautiful green stripes. Sarah knew he wasn't poisonous, so she wasn't scared, except when Jack snuck him into her pocket or tucked him under her pillow.

Her big brother Tom was hoping to find an orphaned bear cub and raise it. He wanted to teach it to do tricks. Sarah wasn't sure how she felt about that. Neither was her mother. Luckily, the only bear cub Tom had found in the woods so far had a devoted mother who chased him off with angry growls. Tom had come running home. He looked scared himself, although he said later that he wasn't really.

Everyone, even little Caroline, was very busy with chores. There were no stores where they lived in the woods of Upper Canada in 1836. Sarah and her sisters picked wild raspberries and gooseberries and strawberries for jam. They gathered nuts and rose hips in the fall, and greens in the spring for tonics. They helped weed the vegetable garden. Every day Sarah hunted for small branches to break up into kindling for the fire in the big fireplace. And she brought water from the stream in the bucket. Caroline helped to carry it.

Only one thing made Sarah sad; she was afraid. All her brothers and sisters knew it. She was afraid of her shadow if it moved suddenly. She was afraid of being alone in the loft. She always persuaded Caroline to come up with her, because Caroline wasn't afraid of anything—except getting soap in her eyes when she was having her hair washed.

"Sarah Scared Rogers—that should be your name," said Tom one day when they had managed to make her cry three times.

"I'm not scared," said Sarah. "Only a little bit of thunderstorms."

"And bees too," said Susanna. "Remember the time Tom poked the honey tree with a stick? All the bees came out and chased you. You were crying so hard that you fell into the lake. Tom had to save you from drowning."

"I wish he had left me to drown," Sarah sniffed.

"I hate you all. I'd run away from home, but I'm…"

"Scared" they all shouted.

CHAPTER 2

The Witch Tree

Sarah took her shawl from the peg on the wall by the door and shook it out to make sure that nobody had hidden a mouse or a couple of woolly caterpillars in it. Why couldn't she be brave like everyone else in the family? Papa had been a soldier and had a shiny medal from the king to prove his bravery. When Mama drew birds and flowers in the woods, she never thought twice about the wolves and bears that might be lurking, just waiting to pounce. Tom had once stopped a runaway horse. Caroline had saved her pigeon Coo-coo from being attacked by a dog. Even little Ruff chased squirrels up trees—although he often got stuck on a high branch and had to be rescued.

Her mother was waiting outside, admiring the ever-changing colors of the leaves. "Orange and red and yellow," she said. "Like flames of fire in the distance." They set off along the trail through the woods to the Ojibwa camp.

The sun shone brightly in the clearing, but in the woods it was always dark and silent and full of shadows. They didn't see any animals, but Sarah knew they were there—beneath the ferns, behind the rocks, up among the branches of the trees. She could feel their bright eyes…watching…waiting. But she didn't feel frightened because Mama was with her, talking cheerfully about making matching gowns for her, Susanna and Caroline for Christmas.

"What color should they be?" Mama asked.

"Green like the little frog who lives under the house," said Sarah, "or maybe red like the maple leaves, or…" She stopped. She heard a tapping sound ahead of them. "What's that?"

"It's only a Downy Woodpecker," said her mother.

They reached the halfway point where the trail squeezed between two huge rocks covered in damp moss. Sarah forgot about Christmas dresses and held tightly to her mother's hand. She was sure that some day the rocks would roll together and crush her, flat as a leaf.

Around the next bend in the trail lay the witch tree. Everyone else might think it was just a dead tree with a thick trunk. Sarah knew there was an old witch trapped inside, waiting to catch her in a cage of twisted branches.

As usual, a big black crow was perched on top, cawing hoarsely. Sarah tried to find her courage, but she couldn't.

"Stop shaking, Sarah," said her mother. "It's only a tree. You must try to get over it, you know."

But Sarah shook and shook. The witch tree groaned and creaked and waved its branches. The big bird stared and made what sounded like rude remarks in crow language.

"You don't know what it's like," Sarah said.

"Oh, yes I do," her mother replied.

"How could you?" Sarah asked. "You're not afraid of anything. You go all alone into the woods and stay there for hours, drawing flowers and birds."

Mama laughed. "Do you know what my brothers and sisters called me when I was a little girl like you?"

"No."

"Cowardy-custard Catharine. And I lived in a sleepy little village in Suffolk, not in the Canadian woods where there really are dangerous things if you aren't careful. My big brother Sam used to chase me with snakes, not just put them in my pocket. My sister Agnes would tell me ghost stories after supper. Then she and Sam would hide under my bed, shaking it and moaning."

Sarah felt a little better. Maybe she would be as brave as Mama when she grew up. But it seemed a long time to wait.

Just before they reached the Ojibwa camp, they had to cross the black cedar swamp. Sarah hated it most of all, with its dark waters full of slimy things. Jack liked to scare her with tales of the giant bloodsuckers that lived there.

"They can always tell when you're afraid," he would whisper. "They clamp on even tighter...and they never let go!"

Sarah tried not to think about the slimy things lurking beneath the cold, black water, while the cedar trees swished their boughs at her. She held on tightly to Mama's warm hand, thinking very hard about the new Christmas dresses. They walked safely across and Sarah stopped trembling.

Magic Courage

T hey came to the edge of the lake where the Ojibwa made their camp beside a thick clump of cedars. Sarah saw their birch-bark wigwams sprinkled around the clearing. Swift Beaver, the tribe's chief and Still Water, one of the warriors, were making arrows. Sarah's friend Bright Fire was throwing a tomahawk at a notch in a tree. He and Sarah shared the same birthday—they would both turn ten in November.

His mother, Kiwana, was stirring venison stew in a big kettle, which hung over the fire. Bannock was cooking in the ashes. It smelled delicious. Sarah hoped she would ask them to stay for dinner.

Bright Fire's three little brothers, all dressed in red flannel shirts, were playing with their young deerhound. First they chased him in circles. Then he chased them.

Mama called out to Kiwana, who looked up from her kettle and smiled. She wore scarlet embroidered trousers with fringes because she was the chief's wife. The other women of the tribe had to be content with plain trousers. Sarah thought Kiwana's trousers were very beautiful. She wondered if she could ask for a pair for her birthday.

They went over to the fire. Kiwana kept on stirring the stew but she pointed to a bearskin for them to sit on. The three little boys stared shyly at Sarah and her mother. Then they threw a stick into the woods and ran off after the puppy as he chased it.

Mama held out a willow pattern china bowl that Papa had brought from town after his last trip. "This bowl is for you," she told Kiwana.

Kiwana looked longingly at it. "What do you want for it?" she asked. "You need baskets?"

She lifted the old blanket that served as a door, went into the wigwam and brought out a beautifully woven basket. Mama looked longingly at it. It would be just perfect for carrying paints and paintbrushes. Then she looked at Sarah's feet, with her toes poking out from the tattered moccasins. They were turning blue from the cold.

"I would like new moccasins for Sarah," Mama said. "Good, strong moccasins to keep her feet warm in winter."

Kiwana nodded and went back into the tent. She came out again, carrying a pair. They were deerskin, lined with fox fur and decorated with porcupine quills over the toes. The pattern was of a sunburst. Kiwana had dyed the porcupine quills in glowing colors—orange and green and purple.

"Try them on," Mama said. Sarah slipped her frozen feet into the moccasins. They felt soft and warm. But no matter how she scrunched up her toes, they pinched.

"How do they fit?"

"They're a little small," Sarah admitted. "Maybe they'll stretch." She wanted them desperately, but all the Rogers children had been taught never to tell lies. Even Caroline knew that it was wrong.

Kiwana looked hard at Sarah's feet, as if she were memorizing them. "I will make another pair. Just right," she said. "Come back in four days."

"Run along and play with Bright Fire," her mother said. "Kiwana and I want to talk."

Sarah knew that meant they would sit together and drink tea and laugh and chatter as if they were girls themselves. They would talk for ages about plants. Kiwana could make all sorts of cures — poultices from tree bark and salves from roots. She even used plants to make the bright dyes for her baskets and porcupine quills.

Sarah ran over to join Bright Fire. "Show me your toys," she said.

"Ojibwa warriors don't play with baby things," Bright Fire said. "I will show you my bow and arrow. I can shoot squirrel and pigeon. Soon my father will give me a gun. Then I will shoot bigger animals. I will be a great hunter like my father," Bright Fire added. "I will fear nothing."

"What makes you so brave?" Sarah asked. Perhaps Bright Fire could help her conquer her own fears.

"Can you keep a secret?" he asked. He looked around the clearing to make sure no one was listening.

"Yes," Sarah said. "What is it?"

Bright Fire took something from his deerskin belt. It was a small pouch made of leather. "Here," he said. "This makes me brave."

"May I see it?" Sarah asked. Maybe she could give back the moccasins and have a pouch that would make her brave too — even if she did have cold feet again.

"It is not for girls," Bright Fire said. "It is my medicine bag. It is great magic. My grandfather gave it to me. He is a wise shaman."

"I wish I had something like that." Sarah's grandfather had sent a book of fairy tales from England for her last birthday. It was full of goblins and witches and dragons, so it didn't make her feel a bit braver. Instead, she just had nightmares.

"What's in it?" Sarah tried to open the pouch, but Bright Fire pulled it away with a frown.

But before she could ask again, her mother called. "Sarah!"

It was time to go home.

CHAPTER 4

Duck Hunting

Sarah could hardly wait for the time to pass. Soon Kiwana would finish her new moccasins. It was all she could think about. Even when Tom and Jack jumped from branch to branch in the big maple, pretending they were flying squirrels, she didn't stand under the tree as she usually did, crying, "Come down! You'll fall off and be killed!"

On the third day, Sarah was standing outside, still as a statue, watching the little green frog hopping by. She heard another small sound and a bush moved just beyond the fence. What she saw made her cry out with excitement and run back to the house.

"The Ojibwas!" she called. "The Ojibwas are coming!"

"Hurray!" all her brothers and sisters shouted. They raced to the door and ran outside, past the vegetable garden and the herb garden and the flower garden, past the stream, down to the edge of the woods. Ruff came along too.

Each one wanted to be the first to greet the Ojibwas. They often came to visit. They wouldn't knock on the door. They would walk right into the house and sit down on the floor by the fire. Or they would wander about the room and pick things up and ask what they were.

Swift Beaver and Still Water stepped into the clearing and nodded their heads gravely, while the children bounced around them, all talking at once. Bright Fire smiled at

Sarah. Then he picked Ruff up to stop him from attacking his ankles. The kitten thought his moccasins were two furry enemies attached to his feet.

"Where is Hummingbird?" asked Swift Beaver. The Ojibwas called Mama Hummingbird because she spent so much time painting birds.

"Drawing the last of the flowers in the woods. She hoped there might still be a few gentians and asters." Susanna said.

"Where is Maker of Sweet Sounds?" asked Swift Beaver. This was their name for Sarah's father. He played the flute. The Ojibwas loved to listen to his songs. They would gather around and sit absolutely still while he played. "Home Sweet Home" was their favorite.

"He's gone to town," Jack said.

"Why do you want them?" Tom said.

"We are going duck hunting," answered Still Water. "There are ducks on the lake, many ducks, resting before they fly away for the winter. We must hurry."

"Could I come?"

"I want to come."

"Me too!"

Sarah's brothers and sisters jumped with excitement. They loved to walk through the woods. They had learned to creep almost as quietly as Bright Fire.

Bright Fire looked up at his father. "Please let them come," he said.

"How will Maker of Sweet Sounds and Hummingbird know where they are? " Swift Beaver asked.

"I'll leave a note on the table to tell them," Susanna said. And she ran back to the cabin. A moment later, she was back, breathless. "I left it under the teapot. Mama will be sure to find it when she comes in," she said. "She always makes a cup of wild strawberry-leaf tea while she decides where to hang her new sketches."

A little breeze blew Sarah's brown curls across her face as they set off. There weren't many leaves left on the trees. Soon winter would come to nip her toes even more fiercely. She was glad she would have new moccasins to keep her feet warm. Soon it would be her birthday.

"I'll be brave by then if it kills me," she said quietly to herself. "I wonder if Bright Fire's grandfather would give me a pouch. I'll ask him when we go for the moccasins." But Bright Fire's grandfather was old and bent and silent. Maybe Bright Fire would ask him.

She began to skip along the uneven forest path. Tom frowned at her, and she remembered that she must be quiet. She might scare away the ducks.

The Feathered Fleet

When they reached the lake, they found the canoes were ready. The Ojibwas had covered them with leafy branches. The canoes looked like small, floating islands. Even the smartest duck wouldn't know there were people inside.

Jack, Susanna and Caroline got into the first branch-covered canoe with Swift Beaver. Sarah and Tom got into

the second canoe with Bright Fire and his father. Quietly they slipped their cherry-wood paddles into the water.

The leafy islands slid quietly through the calm water. Sarah pushed aside one of the branches and poked her head out.

There were the ducks. They floated on the water like feathered ships in a safe harbor. Their heads were green and white and blue. One duck was standing on its head in the water, looking for a fish to eat.

The canoes moved toward the ducks. Closer and closer they came. Still Water and Swift Beaver lifted their paddles out of the water and put them down inside the canoes. Noiselessly they picked up their guns.

Suddenly Sarah was scared again. She liked the feathered fleet that drifted so calmly on the sparkling blue water. She didn't want to see the ducks torn and bleeding, and the blue water slowly turning red.

"No!" she cried. She stood up in the midst of the branches in the canoe. "Stop! Don't shoot! Fly away, ducks!" The canoe rocked back and forth in the water. Sarah nearly fell overboard, but Bright Fire grabbed her skirt and held her back.

The ducks squawked and fluttered, and flew away from the dangerous islands. Swift Beaver and Still Water put their guns back in the canoes. They picked up their paddles and turned the canoes toward the shore. They tied up the canoes, landed, and silently climbed out.

Sarah climbed out too. Miserably she stood beside the canoes, waiting for them to scold her. But they didn't say a word, not even Bright Fire. They gave her a long, stern look, put their guns over their shoulders and strode back to the trail through the woods. Now Sarah felt even worse. It would have been better if they had roared and turned bright red with temper. That was the way Papa acted when they did something wrong. He always calmed down later and apologized for losing his temper. This made them feel sorry for misbehaving.

But on the way back home, her brothers and sisters said enough to make up for the Ojibwas' silence.

"There you go again!" Tom said. "Why do you always spoil things? Now we won't have roast duck for dinner."

"I don't care," said Sarah—although she did.

"You might have fallen overboard and drowned," Susanna scolded. "What would we have told Mama?"

"You were just scared," Jack said.

"Scared Sarah," said Caroline.

When Sarah and her angry brothers and sisters got home, they found their mother drinking a cup of wild strawberry-leaf tea and admiring her newest picture. It was of a patch of partridgeberries, glowing red against a frame of trailing green leaves.

"I'm going to use these as decorations," she said. "They'll make a beautiful wreath for the mantel over the fire. They remind me of the holly we used to have at Christmas time at home in England." Suddenly she got a crumply look. Sarah knew she was sometimes homesick, thinking of the rambling old house in Suffolk where she had grown up with her brothers and sisters.

Just then, Papa came in from town with a load of supplies, and Mama cheered up and looked like her normal self again.

"It's lucky you brought some food for supper, Papa," said Tom as they sat down to eat that night. "Old Sarah

Scared Rogers chased away all the ducks. Swift Beaver and Still Water will never take us hunting again."

Sarah sat by herself. No one would sit beside her. Ruff tried to sneak up onto her lap, but kittens weren't allowed to come to the table for supper, and he had to get down.

"Never mind, Sarah," said Papa. "It was really quite brave of you to attempt to save the ducks when everyone else wanted to shoot them. There's no harm in having a soft heart."

"I'd call it a soft head," Jack whispered to Susanna, and they both giggled. Sarah's eyes filled with tears.

"Stop teasing, children," Mama said. "I want to go to the Ojibwa encampment tomorrow for the new moccasins. Just because you have been unkind to Sarah, I shall leave you at home to wash the clothes. Sarah, you may come with me. I'm sure if we explain, Swift Beaver and Still Water will understand and take you all hunting again."

The New Moccasins

Sarah went to bed early that night. "I will become brave," she vowed. She squeezed poor Ruff so tightly that he yowled and ran under the bed. She was still awake when the others came up, but she pretended to be asleep.

All that night she dreamed of being brave. Sometimes she was saving the whole family from a burning house. Sometimes she was rescuing Tom from drowning, or saving Caroline from a mad bear. In one dream she rescued all the Ojibwas from a flood.

But when she woke up, she was still the same old Scared Sarah.

She lay in bed and watched the dawn blow in. The cold air crept in through the chinks in the wall where the plaster had fallen out between the logs. A long line of frost straggled along the dark wood, like the uneven stitches that Caroline made on her sampler. Sarah shivered and hid beneath the covers while the wind made strange, creaking noises in the rafters. She wished that everyone would wake up. Even if they were mean, at least they were company.

Right after breakfast, Sarah and her mother set off again for the encampment. "Take care of everything now," Mama told Susanna. "I want all the clothes washed and hung to dry by the time Sarah and I get back from the camp. Don't let Caroline fall in the fire."

Susanna and Tom, Jack and Caroline waved good-bye. They looked sad. There were a great many dirty clothes to be washed — piles and piles of them. Sarah felt sorry they were not coming to the Ojibwa camp.

The wind was still blowing and it was very cold. Sarah pulled her cloak around her. During the last four days the trees had become almost bare, their branches black against the gray sky. A single yellow leaf fell off and drifted to the ground like a small skeleton. Sarah stepped on something hard and squishy, and jumped back with a cry. But it was only a moss-covered rock. The wet mud on the path seeped through the holes in her moccasins. She would be very glad to have the new ones. She wondered what the pattern would be. Then she wondered if Kiwana would be angry because of the lost ducks. Maybe she had stopped making them!

When they arrived, the Ojibwa camp looked just as it had before. Thin curls of smoke were coming from the tops of the wigwams. Swift Beaver and Still Water were finishing a birch-bark canoe. Bright Fire was watching. Kiwana was cooking a fish in the ashes of the fire while the three little boys in their red shirts tried to keep the puppy from stealing it. This time Bright Fire didn't come running over to see her. He seemed not to notice that she was there. But Kiwana smiled—the same friendly person as ever. "Your moccasins are ready," she said. She went into the tent and came out again with a beautiful pair of moccasins.

Sarah tried them on. They were a perfect fit. Her feet felt warm for the first time in ages. "Thank you," she said. "Oh, thank you."

"Off you go and play with Bright Fire," said her mother. "But we can't stay long. The days are getting dark."

Sarah went over to the canoe-makers, feeling shy. Were they still angry with her? Although Swift Beaver and Still Water worked on silently, they did give her a quick smile. But Bright Fire had his back to her. Before she could say hello, he said something to his father. Then he ran off into the woods. As he ran, something fell from his shirt to the ground.

It was his medicine pouch. Sarah picked it up, although she was a little afraid of its magic. She began to run after him to return it. Then she felt cross. Why should I, when he's being so mean? she thought.

She looked around. No one was watching. She tucked the pouch underneath her cloak. "I'm not really stealing it," she muttered, "just borrowing it for a few days. Just to see if it helps me be brave. Anyhow, it will serve Bright Fire right for being so mean to me."

Sarah ran back to the edge of the camp. For some reason, she didn't know why, she didn't feel like saying good-bye to Kiwana or the three little boys and their puppy. "Let's go home," she called to her mother. "It's growing dark. It will be spooky in the woods."

Sarah held the magic pouch tightly under her shawl. Her mother said good-bye to Kiwana and followed her. All the way home Sarah was quiet. She didn't tell her mother that she had borrowed the pouch. The wind blew wet leaves against their cheeks and icy drops of rain slid down their necks. Sarah wondered if it would snow. The branches whipped the dark sky, and something shrieked in the distance. She hoped it was a bird.

CHAPTER 7

Nightmares

Sarah was glad when they arrived home. All the clothes were washed and drying by the fire. Tom, Jack, Susanna and Caroline were playing I Spy with Papa. They seemed glad to see her. No one called her Scared Sarah for the rest of the day.

The magic pouch is working, Sarah told herself. When Sippet, hissing softly, slid across the floor toward her, she didn't scream. Even when Jack dressed up in one of Papa's night-shirts and snuck up behind her when she went out to the root cellar for a string of onions, she wasn't afraid.

Then she went up to bed.

"I wonder what magical things are in the pouch?" she asked Ruff, who was trying to bat it with his paw. Very carefully she opened it, half-afraid that the

magical contents might jump out at her, or cast a spell. What if it turned her into something? she thought. It would probably be a frightened mouse.

But all she found were two pieces of ragged fur, a round white stone, a Blue Jay's feather, and a shiny brown chestnut that was as smooth as Mama's best satin gown. The objects didn't look very powerful. But they had to be.

The others were coming to bed, chasing each other up the ladder, so Sarah hastily popped everything back in the bag and hid it under her pillow.

At first she dreamed happy dreams.

Then they changed. She dreamed that Bright Fire was in great trouble because he had lost his medicine bag. His gods were angry with him. The stones and trees in the woods, who were gods too, turned against him. His hunting bag was always empty.

Bright Fire trembled before the angry gods and was afraid. He had to walk alone through the woods, hunting for berries. His three little brothers didn't want to play with him. Even the puppy snarled when he threw a stick for it.

When Sarah woke up the next morning, she was so pale that her mother asked if she was sick. "You must stay in bed today and take some wintergreen tea," she said.

As soon as her mother had gone downstairs to make the tea, Sarah got up and dressed. She put on her new warm moccasins and her cloak. Then she took the magic pouch from under the pillow.

She was scared to death but she knew what she had to do.

She heard Mama go to the herb garden for the wintergreen. Sarah crept downstairs and went quietly outside. She hid behind a big tree stump until her mother had gone back inside the log house. Then she ran as fast as she could through the woods.

Sarah was going to the Ojibwa camp alone.

She knew she must give the magic pouch back to Bright Fire. His gods would not be angry with him and his hunting bag would be full again. She hoped that his gods would not be angry with her for stealing the pouch. I must give it back, she thought, even if I have to be Scared Sarah forever. It isn't fair to take someone else's courage.

Sarah's feet were warm in the new moccasins, but her fingers were cold. She ran faster and faster, not daring to watch the strange shapes that lurked in the dark woods. She hoped they were only tree stumps and big stones. But she couldn't be sure. What if they were some of Bright Fire's gods? What if they were going to punish her? In her family, stealing was even worse than lying.

And then Sarah felt small, scratchy fingers grabbing at her. She tripped and banged her knee on what turned out to be a root. Something suddenly burst out of the underbrush. But it was only a chipmunk. It ran across the path and up a tree, where it sat, scolding her. She was so relieved that it wasn't something big, that Sarah just laughed.

She came to the bend in the trail. There stood the dead tree—the witch tree with its long twisted branches. Today it creaked like an old gate. The big black crow was cleaning his feathers. He stopped, stared down at her and squawked.

Sarah Thief, Sarah Thief, he seemed to say.

CHAPTER 8

Wild Grapes and Scarlet Berries

W hen Sarah reached the Ojibwa camp, she saw Bright Fire shooting at a tree with his bow and arrow. He didn't look frightened or sad at all. Or cross. "Hello, Sarah," he said. "You were here only yesterday. Have you come for more moccasins?"

Sarah gulped. She felt worse than ever. He hadn't noticed that it was lost! She wondered if she could just quietly put the magic pouch in the wigwam and let Bright Fire think that he had left it there. No, she must tell him that she had taken it.

"Here is your medicine bag," she said. She took it out from under her shawl and held it toward him. "I found it on the ground yesterday when you were running away from me."

"I wasn't running away from you," Bright Fire said, looking surprised. "My father heard a noise in the woods and told me to find out if it was a deer. When I came back, I wondered where you had gone."

Sarah felt worse than ever. "I dreamed all night that your gods were angry with you and that your hunting bag was empty. It was wrong for me to steal your courage. I'm sorry. Please forgive me."

Bright Fire looked sternly at Sarah. "It was wrong," he said.

Sarah lowered her eyes in shame. He would no longer be her friend, and she would be Scared Sarah forever. She didn't know which was worse.

Then she heard Bright Fire...laughing!

"Why are you laughing?" she said. "Don't you want your magic pouch? I came all alone through the woods to bring it to you. I was so frightened."

"This pouch has no power," said Bright Fire. "It is only a game. My friends and I play that we are shamans." He looked around the clearing to be sure that no one was listening. "Do not tell anyone. I will get in trouble."

He looked a little frightened himself.

Bright Fire picked up the bundle. "I have no need of magic pouches to be brave." He looked at her with an expression she had not seen before. "You have no need, Sarah. You came through the woods all alone to help a friend. I think you had no fear then."

Sarah didn't like to tell him that she had been scared stiff. She didn't tell him that she had thought every tree and stone was an angry god.

But she did come alone, she realized. She could never have done that before. Maybe, just as Mama said, she might be getting braver as she got older. Or maybe Bright Fire was wrong and the pouch was a little bit magical.

"I will walk home with you," Bright Fire said. "I will come to tell them all how brave you are."

As they walked through the woods, Sarah saw that the sun had come out and was shining through the bare, black branches. It lit up the wild grapes and scarlet berries that twined around the fallen tree trunks. She hadn't noticed them before. Soon November would come. She and Bright Fire would be ten. Perhaps she could persuade Mama to have a birthday party and invite everyone. Papa could play his flute and they would have a big cake with maple syrup icing.

Sarah and Bright Fire made up a song. They sang it as they walked along the path, past trees and stones that looked like trees and stones...not unfriendly gods.

Who's the bravest girl of all?
Sarah Unscared Rogers.
Who answers when the demons call?
Sarah Unscared Rogers.

Sarah could hardly wait to get home and be brave. Even when they reached the witch tree, it looked more like a friendly old tree — a tree that kept them on the right path and stopped them from getting lost in the woods.

Sarah noticed a black feather lying in the pathway. The crow was gone. He must have plucked it out when he was cleaning himself. Sarah picked it up. She knew that she didn't need a magic pouch to give her courage.

Still, she thought she might make one for herself all the same.

Just in case.

GLOSSARY

bannock — a flat bread made of flour, water and fat, cooked in a pan or over a fire.

bearskin — the pelt or hide of a bear, which the Ojibwa used as cloaks and rugs in the winter.

birch bark — the bark of the white birch was used by the First Nations peoples to cover canoes and wigwams. It was also used to make boxes, candles, cups, dishes, and many other objects.

bloodsucker — a leech that attaches itself to people or animals and sucks their blood.

canoe — a narrow, light boat with a pointed bow and stern, usually made with birch bark over a wooden frame.

chink — a narrow opening. In log houses the spaces were filled with mud or moss.

cranberries — a tart, red berry found in swamps or bogs. They are used for relishes, salads, pies, sauces for Thanksgiving turkeys, and decorations.

encampment — a place to camp. Many of the First Nations peoples were nomadic — they roamed from place to place. Whenever they settled in one spot for a season or two, they made a new village in which to live.

gooseberries — round, sour green berries. They are used for jam, pies, sauces, and a traditional dessert — called a "fool" — a mixture of cream and berries.

medicine bag — or medicine bundle. A collection of objects often wrapped in hide, which was believed to give its owner mysterious powers and protection.

moccasin — a soft shoe made of leather from deerskin. Moccasins were often decorated with embroidered or beaded designs and trimmed with fur. The word "Ojibwa" comes from the Algonquin word "otchipwa," which means "to pucker," like the special wrinkled seams of Ojibwa moccasins.

Ojibwa — a First Nations tribe.

Ojibwas — members of that tribe. At one time, the Ojibwa nation stretched from Michigan to Wisconsin, Minnesota and Ontario. They were also known as Ojibway, Ojibwae or Chippewa.

partridgeberries — partridges really do like to eat these bright red berries which ripen late in the fall. Partridgeberry jam is still very popular in Newfoundland.

porcupine quills — the sharp, hollow spines of the porcupine were used in decoration on many articles made by the First Nations people.

poultice — a paste of bread or meal or mustard, softened and heated, spread on a cloth and put on sore muscles or the chest to relieve a cold.

reeds — the stems of tall, slender grasses that grow in wet or marshy land. The firm stems were often used in basketwork.

root cellar — a covered underground pit used to store long-lasting crops like carrots, potatoes, turnips and apples.

rose hips — the ripened fruit of a rose bush. The seeds of the rose hip can be ground and used to make healthy teas and syrups.

salve — an ointment of fat or butter that was spread on a sore spot, wound or burn.

sampler — little girls were taught to sew by making a sampler—a piece of cloth embroidered with different stitches. A first sampler would have numbers and the alphabet as well as simple pictures. Older girls would embroider mottoes, a poem, or verses from the Bible, along with their name and the date.

shaman — the First Nations people looked up to these guides who were thought to have magical powers. The shaman was supposed to have the ability to move between the spirit world and the real world; and they could predict the outcome of a hunt, or find lost objects. It was believed that a bad shaman, or sorcerer, could cast spells.

string of onions — onions with the dried stems woven together in a long "string."

Suffolk — a county in the eastern part of England, bordered by the North Sea.

tomahawk — a light axe used by the First Nations people as a weapon or tool. To "bury the tomahawk" means to make peace.

Upper Canada — part of the Colony of British North America (established in 1791) which is now the Province of Ontario. In 1841, it was joined with Lower Canada (Quebec) to become the Province of Canada. From 1791 on, the colony was commonly referred to as Canada, and its people, Canadians.

venison — meat from the flesh of a deer.

wigwam — a home made with bent saplings stuck in the ground and tied together to make a frame, then covered with bark or animal skins. The Ojibwa built wigwams in both the dome and cone shapes, with an opening in the roof to let the smoke from a campfire escape.

willow pattern — an old china design that is still popular. It is blue on a white background, with pictures of a willow tree, pagodas and a bridge over a river.

SUGGESTED READING

FOR PARENTS AND TEACHERS

To find out more about the settlers of Upper Canada, I'd recommend the following titles:

Moodie, Susanna. *Roughing it in the Bush*. Toronto, McClelland and Stewart, New Canadian Library Edition, 1996.

Traill, C.P. *Canadian Wild Flowers Illustrated by Agnes Fitzgibbon*. Montreal, John Lovell, 1869.

Traill, C.P. *The Backwoods of Canada*. Toronto, McClelland and Stewart, New Canadian Library Edition, 1996.

Traill, C.P. *Canadian Crusoes. A Tale of the Rice Lake Plain*s. Edited by Rupert Scheider, Ottawa, Carleton U.P., 1986.

Gray, Charlotte. *Sisters of the Wilderness*. Toronto, Penguin Books of Canada, 2000.

Langton, Anne. *A Gentlewoman in Upper Canada: The Journals of Anne Langton*. Edited by H.H. Langton, 7th ed. Toronto, Clarke, Irwin, 1975.

I N D E X

INDEX

M
magic, 22, 39, 41, 46, 47
magic pouch *see* medicine bag
medicine bag, 22, 38, 39, 41, 44, 46, 47
moccasins, 9, 20-21, 37

O
Ojibwa camp, 17, 19-22, 37
Ojibwa visit, 25-26
Ojibwa warriors, 21

P
pets, 10, 19, 32-33
plants, 21
playing, 19, 21, 39, 46
porcupine quills, 20, 21
pouch *see* medicine bag
poultices, 21
power *see* magic
preserves, 9

R
reeds, 7
root cellar, 9, 39
rose hips, 10

S
salves, 21
shame, 46
sickness, 42
songs, 26, 47, 49

spell, 41
stealing, 38, 44, 46
Suffolk *see* England
swamp, 15-16

T
tea, 21, 27, 32, 42
teasing, 33
telling lies *see* lying
temper *see* anger
tomahawk, 17
tonics, 10
trees, 10, 27, 36
see also witch tree
trousers, 19

U
Upper Canada *see* Canada

V
venison stew, 17

W
washing clothes, 36, 39
water, 10
wigwam, 17, 20, 37
wild berries *see* berries
wild grapes, 47
witch tree, 13, 15, 44, 49
woods, 10, 13, 15, 44

BIOGRAPHY

MURIEL WOOD was born in Kent, England. She obtained her diploma in design and painting at the Canterbury College of Art before immigrating to Canada. Since the early 1960's, her artwork has appeared in many places: magazines, books, stamps, porcelains and posters. In addition, she has displayed her paintings in a number of group and one-woman shows. Her children's books include L.M. Montgomery's *Anne of Green Gables,* Margaret Laurence's *The Olden Day's Coat* and *Apples and Angel Ladders* by Irene Morck. A former instructor at the Ontario College of Art and Design in Toronto, Muriel now draws and paints full time. She lives with her husband and two cats in Port Hope, Ontario.

BIOGRAPHY

MARY ALICE DOWNIE was born in Alton, Illinois on Abraham Lincoln's birthday. She grew up in Toronto, Ontario, where she obtained a degree in English literature at the University of Toronto. From there she worked for a national magazine, medical journal, and the Canadian branch of Oxford University Press. She also worked as a film, play and book reviewer. In 1968 Mary Alice's first book, with Barbara Robertson, was *The Wind Has Wings: Poems from Canada.* Since then she has gone on to publish over twenty-five books, including *Honor Bound, Snow Paws, Danger in Disguise* and *Bright Paddles.* Mary Alice lives with her husband in Kingston, Ontario, where they have two homes—one in the city, and one on an island in the Rideau Canal Waterway.